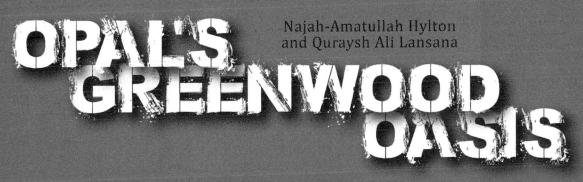

# OPAL'S GREENWOOD OASIS

Najah-Amatullah Hylton
and Quraysh Ali Lansana

Illustrated by
Skip Hill

2021 The Calliope Group, LLC

Copyright © 2021, Najah-Amatullah Hylton
Copyright © 2021, Quraysh Ali Lansana
Copyright © 2021, Skip Hill

Published in the United States by The Calliope Group, LLC
Tulsa, Oklahoma
Hardcover
ISBN: 978-1-7336474-4-1
Library of Congress Control Number: 2020944756

Hello. My name is Opal Brown. I live in Greenwood. That's part of the city of Tulsa in the state of Oklahoma. I just finished third grade here in 1921.

On Mondays in Greenwood, all the children wake up and eat breakfast. We grab our books, get on our bikes and ride off to school. We learn reading, writing, and arithmetic, music and art and physical education.

While the children are at school, the mothers cook and clean. They wash and cut hair at Madame CJ's.

They serve sodas and work the counter at Williams's drugstore. They help customers measure their sizes at the department stores. They make dinner and iron laundry at their own homes.

While the children and the mothers are busy, the fathers are working hard, too. They read long papers at the law office.

They load heavy groceries and fix cars. They help sick patients and clean dirty teeth. They run hotels and shops.

On Saturdays in Greenwood, children run and ride through the streets. We go on errands for our parents. We ask for nickels and dimes to buy sodas and burgers. Grown-ups sit on porches and at lunch counters catching up. Families go to the matinee at the Williams Dreamland Theater.

On Sundays in Greenwood just about everybody goes to church. We dress up fancy and behave our very best even though it's crowded and hot. We sing hymns and listen while the pastor preaches. When service is over, we walk home to eat cold cut sandwiches and salad for lunch while the women cook up big dinners.

In Greenwood, we have everything we need, and it might surprise you to know that everyone looks like me.

This week it's Memorial Day, so everything but the drugstore is closed. Even Williams's theater shut down at noon because the community picnic starts at one o'clock.

Memorial Day, Greenwood, 1921

Early in the morning, I was pulling empty cardboard boxes from the toting truck for Mama to pack food. Daddy had to go to the car repair shop to work on the truck before the picnic. My big brother, Sammy, left early as always. He delivers the newspaper every day except Christmas.

Daddy and I waved at Dick Rowland as he left his Auntie Damie's.

"See ya later, Dick," Daddy called, walking outside.

"Have a good day, sir!" Dick said back.

"Daddy, isn't Dick going the wrong way? The picnic is that way."

"No, he's going to work at the shoeshine parlor on Main."

"Where's that?" I asked. "I thought everything was closed today."

"Everything in Greenwood is closed. The white folks don't close all their stores for Memorial Day."

"Why not?"

"Over here, we like to celebrate holidays altogether. They do things a lot different on that side of town."

"How do they do things?"

"Opal, that's a long talk for another day."

Later, I was sitting at the table, with a book on one side, and snap peas in front of me.

"I don't see my cinnamon." Mama kept reaching behind spice jars and banging cans on the counter. "And now it'll take too long for me to go get it!"

"We forgot it at the store? I can go on my bike!" I shouted and jumped up.

"Are you sure you're ready? If something happens, what will you do?"

"Ask the closest grown-up for help."

Mama nodded and grabbed her purse. She tucked some money into the small pocket of my dress.

"Okay, you go straight there and back, do you hear?"

I started down the block with a huge smile on my face. I had spent the long weekend practicing bike riding with Daddy. Even though it was hard, I remembered his calm voice telling me I could do it. That made me feel proud.

Turning the corner easy now, I saw Dr. Bridgewater's office on my right and the Tulsa Star newspaper on my left. As I came close to Madame CJ's, old Mrs. Little called out to me.

"Opal Brown! Is that you riding down here all alone?"

"Yes ma'am! I'm fetching cinnamon from the store for my mama."

"You be careful, you hear?" She waved me on but looked worried.

"Yes, ma'am. I will."

I rode past the Royal Hotel and Reverend Netherland's barber shop, the theater and Vernon AME. Far up ahead, I could see men setting out tables for the picnic, covering them with potato sack cloths. I pulled up to Mr. Mann's store and went inside.

"Opal Brown! Did you just ride here all by yourself?"

"Yes, Mr. Mann, I did. Mama needs cinnamon quick. We forgot it on Friday," I said like a grown-up.

"Where's your daddy?" He asked.

"At the shop. Had to fix the toting truck tires before the picnic." I carried the small jar to the counter and dug the money out of my pocket.

Mr. Mann added up the cost and took my money. "And I guess Sammy's at the paper?"

"Yes, sir. The news doesn't take days off." I told him what Sammy always says.

Mr. Mann chuckled without smiling. "Alright then. Let me wrap this up good since you're carrying it in that bike basket. That way, if you fall, you won't lose any. See you get back home safe, Miss Opal."

"Yes, sir, thank you. See you at the picnic!" I smiled big and waved.

I tied the basket ribbons around the paper sack. Then I started off slowly.
I waved at my best friend Esther as I pedaled past Mr. Berry's jitney service and Mr. Jackson's funeral home. I passed the houses of the Joneses, the Rowland-Fords, the Smiths and then the Millers right before our house.

I ran inside with Mama's cinnamon.

"Oh good! Just in time. Any longer and the pies wouldn't have time to bake." Mama started mixing right away. "Are you alright? Did you fall?"

"I toppled once but I didn't fall down."

"That's good."

Around 11:30, Daddy came back in from work. His eyebrows were scrunched up like he was thinking real hard, but I couldn't wait to tell him my news. He hugged me tight around the shoulders and then went to wash up.

Right after Sammy came in, everyone started grabbing boxes and carried them to the truck. Then, I saw Dick Rowland running toward Auntie Damie's.

"Hey look!" I said. "Why's Dicky running like that? He looks like he's being chased."

"When I was delivering, I heard a few men talkin' about some trouble at the parlor where Dick shines shoes," Sammy told us. Daddy gave Mama that 'grown-ups only' look. He looked between Sammy and me.

"Not quite, son. The men have been talking about how something happened between Dick and that white girl who works the elevator at the Drexel. No one's sure what really happened, but I don't want you two talking about it anymore, especially at this picnic."

Farm Fre
TOMATO

"Yes, sir," we both said together.

"Alright. That's the last of it." Mama put a big smile on her face and we all piled into the truck.

When we got to the picnic, I helped carry boxes. Mama and I laid out our blanket next to Esther and her family. After making our plates, I sat with my best friend and told her all about my first ride alone.

My prize was a big slice
of blueberry pie.

## What Happened to Opal's Oasis?

Tulsa Historical Society & Museum

Just hours after the events described in this book, Opal's beloved Greenwood would be destroyed by one of the worst acts of racial violence in American history known as the Tulsa Race Massacre. Thirty-six blocks of homes and businesses gone. Countless lives lost. Greenwood would transform from one of the most prosperous Black communities in the country to a ruin. But the people and families of Greenwood were strong. Many would return and rebuild. By 1942, over 200 Black owned businesses would again reside in Greenwood.

You can learn more about Greenwood and the history of the Tulsa Race Massacre at thecalliopegroup.com/product/opal.

# About the **Authors**

**Najah-Amatullah Hylton** has been writing since she was a little girl in school. She always had fun acting in school plays and singing in church choirs. Now she teaches reading, writing, stories and poems to high school students. She also gets to write and read her own poems with her friends like Jabee. They made a hip hop album together called "Black Future." Najah likes to make videos that help people, especially other teachers and students.

**Quraysh Ali Lansana** loves to read, write and imagine. His active imagination often results in books, events and classroom lesson plans. Known by many as "Q," he has written nine poetry books, three textbooks, four children's books, and has co-written a book to help teachers teach poetry. Q has also edited eight anthologies of literature. He loves making books and loves to study history, politics and learn about different cultures. Q also loves music, art and likes to learn and laugh.

Q also loves to teach, and he has taught in elementary schools, high schools and universities across the country, including Tulsa, Chicago, and New York City. Q's favorite writers are Gwendolyn Brooks, Lucille Clifton and James Baldwin.

# About the **Illustrator**

**Skip Hill** is a mixed-media visual artist in Tulsa, Oklahoma whose art is in public and private collections throughout the U.S., Europe, and Latin America.

His early inspiration for making was established in childhood through a love for reading and when his father introduced Skip to the collage works of Romare Bearden (1911–1988). Beyond his artistic innovation, Bearden's activism and commitment to the Civil Rights Movement, influenced Skip Hill's commitment to using Art and art education as a vehicle for affirming positive personal and social change.

That commitment and inspiration is at the heart of Skip Hill's process and in every line of the illustrations for Opal's Greenwood Oasis.

Skip worked previously with Quraysh Ali Lansana as the illustrator for A Gift from Greensboro (Penny Candy Books, 2016).